TERRY DEARY

Saxon Tales

The Lord Who Lost His Head

Illustrated by
Tambe

BLOOMSBURY EDUCATION
AN IMPRINT OF BLOOMSBURY
LONDON OXFORD NEW YORK NEW DELHI SYDNEY

Bloomsbury Education
An imprint of Bloomsbury Publishing Plc

50 Bedford Square
London
WC1B 3DP
UK

1385 Broadway
New York
NY 10018
USA

www.bloomsbury.com

BLOOMSBURY and the Diana logo are trademarks of Bloomsbury Publishing Plc

Terry Deary and T⌐   :nts Act, 1988,

Every reasonable (d in this book,
but if any have   rom them.

This is a work   nation and
any

All rights res⌐   any form
or by any means   information
storage (shers.

No responsibility   ng from action
as a result of the material in this publication can be accepted by Bloomsbury or the author.

A catalogue record for this book is available from the British Library.

ISBN
PB: 978 1 4729 2924 2
ePub: 978 1 4729 2925 9
ePDF: 978 1 4729 2926 6

2 4 6 8 10 9 7 5 3 1

Typeset by Amy Cooper Design
Printed and Bound by CPI Group (UK) Ltd, Croydon CR0 4YY

This book is produced using paper that is made from wood grown in managed, sustainable forests.
It is natural, renewable and recyclable. The logging and manufacturing processes conform to the
environmental regulations of the country of origin.

To find out more about our authors and books visit www.bloomsbury.com. Here you will find extracts,
author interviews, details of forthcoming events and the option to sign up for our newsletters.

Contents

1

The Peasant

'Never trust a lord.' That's what my dad always said. 'Ooooh,' he used to rage. 'They will trick you and trap you and dirty-deal and double-cross you. They will treat you like mud on their boot until they want something from you. And then... *then*... they will treat you like a king.' He looked at me from under his thick and fierce eyebrows. 'Or, in your case, Marian, a princess.'

Mother stirred the pot of porridge and dropped in some scraps of a rabbit that Dad had snared in the woods.

'I'd like to be a princess,' I sighed. 'I bet they don't have porridge for dinner every day.'

'With rabbit, don't forget,' Mum snapped. 'Your dad spent half the night setting those rabbit traps.' She wiped the sweat from her brow, sweat that had been dripping into the rabbit porridge. It would sit there and simmer all day.

'*Most* of the night,' Dad grumbled. 'Just so my little princess could have some meat with her meal. And what does she say?'

Mum put in, with a whine in her voice,

'Urrrr. I have to have porridge for dinner every day.' I think the whine was supposed to be me.

'Urrrr,' Dad echoed. 'I have to have porridge for dinner every day.'

'Sorry Dad,' I muttered.

'I should think so too,' Mum said. 'Poor Dad. He's probably too tired to go to work in the fields, aren't you, love?'

'I am, my love. Breaking my back, pulling up weeds under the burning sun and the pouring rain,' he groaned.

'Yes, dad,' I said. 'But you can't be pulling up weeds under the rain *and* the sun,' I added.

His eyebrows met in the middle as he glared at me. 'Sun one day, rain the next. And why? I ask you? Why?'

I knew the answer to that one. 'So King Offa can stuff his grain stores full of food while we go hungry, Dad.'

The eyebrows rose. 'How did you know I was going to say that?'

'Because you say it every day. Sometimes ten times a day.'

He sniffed. 'Well I wasn't going to say it this time. Why do I labour in the fields? So my daughter can moan on about how boring her dinner is. Well let me tell you, princess, when I was a young churl we went for days without meat... weeks... months...'

'Years?' I asked.

'Don't be cheeky,' Mum said, 'or you'll have no dinner at all.'

'Sorry Mum,' I said. She slopped porridge into my wooden bowl. It smelled good. The day before, Dad had patched a crack in the wooden walls with some cow dung and that would smell quite strong until it dried. It didn't put me off my food.

Mum went back to her weaving and Dad ate slowly. He did that so he didn't have

to work a moment sooner than he had to. Most days the village chief had to bang on our door to get Dad out.

But that morning it was just a light rattle on the door. 'I'm coming,' Dad groaned. 'Just making sure our Marian has enough to eat.'

The door creaked open and Mistress Longmeadow put her head around it. 'It's only me.'

'Oh,' Dad said with a sigh. 'What do you want?'

'I've got news,' the old woman said. She was so old she creaked when she moved. Dad said she was over forty years old.

'Yes, it'll be something exciting like it was last time. What did you barge in to tell us? The priest had a hole in his shoe or something.'

Mistress Longmeadow grinned and showed her gums. 'No. Even more exciting than that. The whole village is meeting outside the chief's house. You wouldn't believe what Thane Ethelbert's done now. You wouldn't be-*lieve* it.'

2
The Churls

Bertram was chief churl of Clun village: a thin-faced man with a mouth that turned down in a wide curve, like a pale grey rainbow. 'What's it all about?' people were muttering. There were village meetings most evenings in the torchlight of Bertram's hall. But not in the daytime when we were supposed to be working.

'Is every free man of Clun here?' Bertram cried.

'Aye, and the free women too,' Mistress Longmeadow piped.

Bertram threw out his chest as far as it would go... which was about as far as your nose from your face. 'Thanes of Clun, we are gathered here today with serious news.'

The crowd gasped, even though they didn't know what the news was. 'As you know, King Ethelbald was killed last year. His bodyguards killed him.'

'Served him right,' someone laughed. 'Nasty old goat.'

'And now,' Bertram went on, 'our country is ruled by Offa.'

'Hah,' Dad whispered to me, 'they say Ethelbald was killed on the orders of Offa. He sort of polished him Offa. Hurr, hurr.'

Dad loved riddles and bad jokes. Nobody else did. Sad Dad.

'Shush,' someone hissed at Dad. 'This is serious.'

'Offa is a powerful king,' Bertram said. 'He is so mighty he plans to build a great wall and ditch all the way along the border with Wales.'

'Is that to keep the Welsh out or to keep us in?' Dad laughed. No one else did. Bertram ignored him.

'We have to pay him a tribute every year, as you know. It pays for his army that protects us from the wild men of Northumbria and the Welsh tribes.'

'It also pays for his feasting and his fine wooden palace with feather beds,' Mistress Longmeadow screeched.

'And his hunting hounds and hawks,' Tolan the blacksmith grumbled.

'And his fat treasure chests full of our gold and silver,' Sheena the shepherd's wife complained.

The meeting was getting noisy and out of control. Bertram had to screech to be heard. 'We know all this. Be quiet.'

The grumblers rumbled into silence. Bertram said, 'It isn't just us churls that think Offa is harsh. There are some among our lords and thanes that are unhappy too.'

'So why don't they do something about it?' Tolan demanded.

Bertram gave a wise nod. 'Oh, but they are, my dear blacksmith. They are. I have here, in my purse something that could bring death to us all.'

'What is it? A bottle of poison?' Sheena asked.

'No,' Bertram said. Then he waited. No one was arguing or shouting now. He waited a little longer. He slipped a hand into his purse.

He pulled it out and made a fist. As the villagers pushed forward to get a better look he unfolded his fingers.

'Ahhhh,' the crowd sighed. Some looked

greedily on the gold coin, and some looked disappointed.

'Is that all?' I asked.

He held the coin between his thumb and first finger. 'Look closely.'

I looked. Oh. Yes, that could bring death to us all.

3
The Coin

Offa was the king. His head was on the coins. That was the way it had always been. But the head on this gold coin wasn't Offa. 'Who is it?' I asked Bertram.

'It's our local thane. Ethelbert.'

'He can't do that,' Mistress Longmeadow squeaked. 'Only the king can make coins.'

'Ah,' Bertram said. 'That's because Ethelbert fancies himself as king. He's a rebel.'

'He must be mad. King Offa will get an army and kill him,' Dad said.

'And Ethelbert will get an army to defend himself,' I replied. 'And where will Ethelbert get men to fight for him?'

My dad groaned. 'He'll make his churls fight for him. He'll make us go to war.'

I nodded. 'So it's simple really. We fight for Ethelbert and Offa's soldiers will kill us. Or we don't fight for Ethelbert and Ethelbert will kill us. We get to choose.'

'I choose to live,' Tolan the blacksmith said.

'So what do we do?' my mum asked him.

Tolan shrugged his massive shoulders and mumbled, 'I don't know.'

'I do,' I said. 'We keep quiet about the coins. We don't try to spend them outside of Ethelbert's land. Tolan can make a new stamp and stamp all the rebel coins with Offa's head.'

'I can make the stamp,' Piers the priest called from the back of the crowd. 'I can make an iron stamp. I worked with iron when I was a monk.'

And suddenly the crowd was cheerful again.

'Of course as soon as we have the coins stamped with Offa's head we can take them to him and pay our village taxes,' Bertram said. They are due this week.'

'Ah.' A sigh. The crowd grew gloomy.

The chief thane pointed at my dad. 'You, Norris. It's your turn to take Clun's taxes to the court of King Offa.'

'I'm too busy,' Dad spluttered.

'It's your duty,' Bertram said sternly. 'We work for one another in Clun. Everyone must play their part. It's your turn.'

Dad grumbled some more but the other villagers had melted away like summer snow and there was no one else to do the dangerous deed.

'Oh, Norris,' Mum sighed that night,

when sunset brought an end to the work in the fields. 'Oh, Norris. I hope you come home safe. But if you don't come back don't worry. Bertram's wife died last year and I think he's got his eye on me to take her place.'

Father spluttered and blustered, 'I'm not dead yet.'

'Of course not, dearest. I'm just saying...'

'Here,' Dad exploded. 'Is that why he's sending me into danger? Is he hoping I'll

wake up dead so he can get his hands on my wife? It's not fair, that isn't. Well I'm going to come back alive. That'll show him,' Dad raged and he stormed off to sleep in the cattle pen at the end of the room.

Mum smiled at me in the amber glow of the dying fire. 'So how would you like Bertram as your new dad, Marian?'

'Not a lot, Mum. Not a lot.'

4

The Bandits

The village might just survive if we paid Offa our taxes. Everyone hurried off to do their duties. That day I was milking the goats to make cheese. Dad took the

cart with the village ox and Bertram gave him the coins that Tolan the blacksmith had stamped with the head of Offa.

I waved at him as he drove past the field where I was working. He looked glum. When he came home that night with no ox, no cart and no money he told us his story. This is how Dad told it...

I came to the woods where the Welsh bandit, Robert, and his merry men live. They live in caves in the woods and they know when the villages pay their taxes to Offa. So I knew they'd be hiding in the trees, waiting to rob me. They would probably kill me, I thought.

So I came up with a clever plan. I decided to take the road through the middle of the woods. If they were waiting at the edge, watching the main road, then I'd be sneaking round behind them.

Brush and branches scraped my face; blackbirds chattered and told the world that I was passing through. I tried holding my breath to get through without a sound but wheels creaked and the ox snorted and twigs on the path cracked under my wheels.

Sadly, Robert's bandits weren't on the edge of the woods waiting for tax wagons. They were in their lair in the middle of the woods counting the coins from the villagers they'd already robbed. And I rode into the middle of them. Oh, dear.

Of course I wasn't afraid. Oh no, not me. 'Good afternoon,' I said with a cheerful smile.

A man got up from the camp fire. He was as solid as an oak tree and nearly as tall. He was dressed in fine (but stolen) clothes. His cut-throats put arrows into their bows and aimed them at me. I did think I could leap

29

down from my cart and fight them all with my bare fists. As I say, I wasn't the least bit afraid. But there were fifty of them... well, twenty... well, five that I could see. There could have been fifty in the caves.

One had red hair and freckles and crooked teeth when he grinned. He was grinning then. 'Looks like a treasure wagon to me, Robert,' he said.

'Very kind of the gentleman to bring it to us, Walter the Red,' the man of oak said. He looked down at me from his tree-top height. 'Drop the money bag on the ground.'

I did as he asked. Well I was only being polite. Robert turned to a man dressed as a monk. In fact, I think he was a monk. 'What shall we do with him, Tuck?' he asked. 'Tie him to a tree and fill him full of arrows, or hang him?'

'We don't have a rope,' the monk answered.

I looked in the back of the wagon where the miller had left stuff from the last time the cart was used. 'I have a rope,' I said.

Robert blinked, then he smiled slow and wide. 'Why thank you. Maybe you'd like to make a noose, tie the end of the rope round the branch of a tree. Put the noose around your neck then kick the ox till it drags the cart from under your feet? It would save us a lot of trouble.'

'Ah. Yes,' I spluttered. I was being so brave I was being careless. 'I have a better idea,' I said.

'Ooooh,' Walter the Red said. 'What's that?'

'Well... when the village fails to deliver the taxes Offa will burn it down. To stop him the villagers will gather another bag of gold. And I will bring it back here for you and instead of one bag you'll have two.'

The fat monk nodded. 'It sounds like a good plan to me.'

The oldest greybeard of the merry men wore fine silks over a body as greasy as mutton fat. 'Sounds like a plan to me.'

The foolish fellow, I thought. As soon as I got back to the village I wouldn't leave it again. If Offa wanted his money he could send a troop of his warriors to Clun to collect it.

I gathered the reins of the ox cart. 'Walk on,' I cried.

'Wait,' Robert said. 'Leave the ox. You can walk home.'

'Why do you need an ox in the forest?'
I asked.

'To eat,' the fat monk snickered and rubbed his belly. 'When you come back with the next bag of gold we'll have some oxtail stew ready for you.'

And so I left the woods and the bandits behind. But at least I'm alive... which is more than the poor ox can say.

*

Mum was not pleased to see Dad come home penniless. But when the villagers gathered that evening, Bertram smiled his upside-down smile. 'Tolan the Blacksmith hasn't finished stamping the gold coins. He just cut up some horseshoes and dropped them in the bag. When Robert opens it he'll find it's full of scrap iron.'

'So I risked my life for nothing?' Dad asked.

'No, you risked your life so the next cart will get through without any trouble,' Bertram said.

'I'm not going back,' Dad said. 'When they find I gave them iron instead of gold they really will hang me and probably fill me full of arrows too.'

Bertram shook his head. 'You're not going back,' he said.

'So who is?' Piers the priest asked.

Bertram jabbed out a skinny finger and pointed at me. 'Marian can go. Even if

the bandits spot her they'll never suspect a girl.'

'And if they do kill her,' Dad grinned, 'it won't matter so much as losing a strong worker like me.'

Thanks, Dad, I thought. Thanks.

5

The Princeling

I set off the next morning. Mum had given me some of her cakes to eat on the journey. If I saw a wild boar on the track I could pelt it with the cakes. They would kill it dead. Mum was not a good cook.

There was no village ox so I pulled a handcart along the rutted and muddy road. Before I could get to the goat field, I saw a boy ride slowly into the village. He had a fine pony and purple velvet clothes with strands of gold woven in. His hair was just

as golden and his face as handsome as a deerhound, with a nose just as long.

'Are you the messenger taking the taxes to Offa?' he asked.

'Are you Robert the bandit?' I asked.

'Do I look like a bandit?' he said, as hurt as if I'd pricked him with my dinner knife.

'My dad says they dress in fine clothes they've stolen from the rich.'

He spread his pale hands – hands that had never worked. 'But under the fine clothes they are dirty and have foul-smelling bodies. Do I smell?'

'No, my lord.' I don't know why I called him that. My lord? He was a boy little older than myself but he looked as fine as the saints that were painted on the church walls.

'I am Kenrick – my name means royal ruler – and I am the son of Lord Ethelbert,' he said.

'The traitor,' I gasped.

Kenrick gave a secret smile. 'Indeed. Offa is a cruel tyrant, my father says. Father thinks he can overthrow Offa and rule in peace.'

'Fine words,' I muttered. 'But how will you rebel?'

Kenrick looked sly. 'All we need is a spy. Someone who will go into the court of King Offa and report on his fortress... the weak places, the way it is guarded and the weapons they have.'

'And if the spy is caught they'd be tortured terribly. Who would do such a dangerous job?' I asked.

'You could,' Kenrick said.

My mouth opened but the wind seemed to have swept my words away. At last I said, 'Why?'

'Because I will give you this purse of gold. You can go into Offa's fortress and

no one will suspect you. I will go with you as your bodyguard.'

He opened the purse and I peered inside. The coins glittered in the weak sunlight. Piers the Priest warned us about greed. 'For the love of money is a root if all kinds of evil,' he roared. I had never loved money... until I saw that glinting beauty calling me. I snatched at the bag.

Kenrick pulled it out of my ready. 'Not until we have done as my father's wishes,' he said. 'Shall we go? I can hitch my pony to your cart and we can ride behind it.

And so we set off to the court of the awful Offa. But first we had to face the bandits.

6

The Villains

When we reached the woods the bandits oozed out of the trees like slime from a slug trail. They blocked the road. Kenrick jumped down from the cart and spread his arms wide in welcome. 'You must be the famous Robert the Good and his Merry Men?'

'Famous?' the one with red hair and freckles said. (He must have been the Walter the Red who Dad told me about.)

'Yes, even though you are Welsh, you

are real heroes in our village,' Kenrick said with a soft whine in his voice. 'Heroes.'

'We are?' the greasy greybeard one asked.

'You are so very kind,' Kenrick went on.

And then I understood his crafty game. 'Yes,' I said. 'You steal from the rich to give to the poor, they say.'

The man of oak, Robert, scratched his head and said, 'We steal from the rich because the poor have nothing worth pinching.'

Kenrick said, 'This poor girl has a sick grandmother who lives in a cottage in the woods. She is taking honey cakes to her.'

'I likes cakes,' the greasy greybeard said. 'Give me a honey cake or I'll cut your throat.'

Nice man. I reached into my bag and handed one to him. It served him right. He opened his mouth wide and the green

teeth bit down on my mother's treat. He cried out. The cake had no tooth-damage but his teeth had cake-damage. 'It broke me tooth,' he wailed and ran off into the shrubs at the edge of the woods to spit blood over the dying leaves. As I said, my mum was not a good cook. And, as I also said, he deserved it.

'Give the girl some money and her granny will tell the world what wonderful gentlemen of the green-wood you all are.'

'And so will the priest,' I put in. 'After all, the love of money is a root of all kinds of evil,' I reminded them.

Robert looked angry. 'Yes, well... we like being evil. And we like our money. So clear off and leave us to rob some idiots.'

Kenrick climbed back onto the cart. The tax money seemed safe. Kenrick had played a clever game. 'Are there many idiots around here?' I asked.

'There are lots and lots and lots of idiots around here,' the fat monk said.

'You're right there,' I said.

Kenrick and I rode off laughing.

*

We reached the fortress of Offa around noon. The mighty wooden walls looked down on us. And so did the guards.

'Are we going to start spying?' I whispered to Kenrick. I wanted that purse of gold as soon as possible.

He shrugged. 'Maybe later. I'll come with you in case you need my help,' he said.

'Help? What help?'

'We'll see,' he murmured. 'You never know.'

We were led to the treasury where Offa's banker sat at a desk, back bent over parchment where he was keeping a record. He wore a fusty and faded black cloak that seemed to wrap itself around the coins on his desk.

I placed my bag of coins on his desk. 'From the village of Clun,' I said. 'Forty-seven gold pieces.'

The man picked up the bag. 'It doesn't feel like forty-seven,' he said.

I groaned. Bertram had tried to cheat Offa... and I was the one who would suffer. I closed my eyes and tried not to weep as the man counted out the coins slowly. 'Forty-two,' he said. 'You are five pieces

short. Do you know what we do to people who try to cheat King Offa?'

'No,' I croaked.

'We slice off their ears, slit their noses and send them back to their village with a troop of our nastiest soldiers. They start cutting off the ears of everyone in the village until the last silver penny is paid.' The banker raised a hand like a claw and called out, 'Guards?'

Three men in coats of mail hurried into

the room. A clawed finger pointed at me and they stepped forward.

A hand reached over my shoulder. A hand with a fine velvet sleeve and a purse. It was Kenrick. His voice was smooth as the velvet. 'Allow me to pay you, sir,' he said quietly. 'We owe the king five more pieces? Here are ten. Give five to the king and...' he winked, '... keep five for yourself, eh?'

The banker licked his lips. 'And who are you?'

'I am Kenrick, son of Ethelbert... he is overlord of the region around Clun. He would hate to hear that one of his churls had her ears cut off.'

I would hate to hear that too... except I wouldn't hear it because I'd have no ears. I was so grateful I could have kissed Kenrick. Though in truth I couldn't have reached his lips with mine because his nose was so very long.

The banker picked up the coin and bit it. It was soft metal – gold. He weighed it in his hand. It  was gold. Then he looked at it and his face turned grey as a February sky.

He looked up at the guards who were still waiting to pounce on me. 'Send for King Offa,' he said.

The guard twitched. 'The king is feasting. He don't like to be disturbed for not nobody and not nothing,' the guard said.

The banker held the coin in his fist. 'He'll want to be disturbed for this.'

7
The King

The king marched into the room, wiping food off his long beard. His eyes were red and like a mad dog who once ran through Clun biting everyone in his way. He seemed to fill the room. He wasn't wearing a crown. I suppose kings never do when they're eating dinner.

'What is it, Selwyn?' he thundered at the banker. The rest of us shrunk back in fear. The man in faded black simply handed over a coin from Kenrick's purse. King Offa snatched it and his red face turned purple. 'What is this? Who dares put his head on a coin in my country?'

'Lord Ethelbert, sire,' Selwyn told him.

'So he wants my throne, does he? He will find it a poor view from the top when I cut off his treacherous head. And who brought these coins to court?' The king's gaze fell on me. 'Was it you, girl?'

'It was I,' Kenrick said.

'And who are you, my strutting peacock?'

Kenrick bowed very low. 'I am Kenrick, sire. Son of Ethelbert.'

For a moment Offa seemed to struggle to breathe. I felt the same. At last the king said, 'The son of the traitor? Are you mad, coming here? You can die alongside your snake of a father,' Offa thundered.

Kenrick held up both hands. 'You do not understand, sire. I came here to warn you what my father is about. He sent me to spy on you. I came here to betray him.'

Offa's red eyes went narrow. 'Why would you want that?'

'Because I am no fool. You are a mighty king and a great warrior. I knew that as soon as you heard about my father's coins you would destroy him and his nest of vipers. I would be killed with the rest of them. Better I tell you now and you may forgive me.'

'Forgive you?'

'And give me my father's lands and fortress and coffers filled with silver and gold.'

Offa placed his face close to Kenrick's.

Then he rested a heavy hand on the boy's shoulder. 'You are ruthless and wicked, young Kenrick.'

'I know,' Kenrick said with a small sigh and a smaller smile.

'You are just the sort of man I need to help me rule my English people and crush our Welsh enemies.'

Kenrick bowed again. 'I am exactly the sort of man you need,' he agreed.

King Offa turned on his heel and was shouting orders for his army to gather even before he'd left the room. 'I will not sleep till the head of Ethelbert is eating dust at my feet,' he yelled.

*

I stayed the night in the fortress, well fed and cared for by Selwyn. After all, I was the friend of the shining young star that was Kenrick.

We rode back the next day towards Clun. At the crossroads our new lord turned to head for his family fortress. The churned mud showed that Offa's army had already ridden that way. Ethelbert's head would be eating dust by now. 'Good day, Marian. I am sure I will see you again when I travel around my towns and villages to meet my churls and thanes.'

'I never got my purse of gold,' I said as he unfastened his pony from the cart and left me to drag it home. 'You promised.'

Kenrick grinned his handsome, saintly

grin. 'I know, Marian. I will not be giving you a single silver penny. And do you know why?'

'Why?'

'Because the love of money is a root of all kinds of evil.'

He mounted the pony and rode off laughing. 'Never trust a lord,' my dad always said. 'They will trick you and trap you and dirty-deal and double-cross you.'

Mum and Dad were happy to see me risk my life. They cared for me no more than for one of the serfs who slaved for the village. The lords would let you down as Kenrick had. The village churls grumbled about their kings and thanes but never did anything. I faced another thirty or forty years of drudgery and misery and marriage to some idle churl. Unless...

When Robert and his men stepped out on the road, later that day, to rob me, I knew where my future lay.

'Your money or your life,' the greybeard said, pointing an arrow at my heart. He needed a good scrub and a well-cooked meal. The others had fine clothes that were ruined with dirt. They had money and all the fine deer-meat they could hunt, but it was badly cooked and joyless.

Still they had one thing that was as priceless as the jewels in any king's golden

crown. Something I'd never had. They had freedom.

'You are the worst outlaws I ever met,' I snapped. 'You need someone with brains to make you the best. In years to come you will be fabled if you have the right leader. You'd be remembered forever as Robert Good and his Merry Men. You will rob the rich and give to the poor. And I am just the maid to lead you,' I said.

'A maid called Marian?' the monk called Tuck said. 'Robert's strong but not very bright. You're right. We need you. I welcome you to our gang.'

I laughed. 'No. I welcome you to my gang.'

And the rest, dear reader, is legend.

END

Epilogue

Offa was King of the Saxon kingdom of Mercia from 757 AD until he died in 796. He took the throne when there was a rebellion against Ethelbald, the previous king. Some say Offa was part of the rebellion. Ethelbald was murdered in the night by his own bodyguards. In those days you could trust no-one.

In his years on the throne, Offa faced a few lords who wanted to take his crown. In 794, Ethelbert rebelled and Offa had him beheaded. It was a cruel world and Offa kept his power because he was crueller than anyone.

Today he is remembered for Offa's Dyke. He had a ditch and wall of earth built to keep the Welsh out of his kingdom. There were constant raids by the Welsh. Some were just robber-bandits and some wanted to conquer English land. Offa's Dyke was a huge effort: 20 metres wide, 2.4 metres high and around 150 miles long. It was so huge there are many stretches that can still be seen today, 1200 years later.

The legend of a good bandit and outlaw band is from ancient times. The best-known story is from the 1300s when he is called Robin Hood of Sherwood Forest. But there were stories of Welsh heroes too... and the women who joined them then led them in their battle against the wicked, grasping, cruel lords.

YOU TRY...

1. HEADS YOU WIN

You are the ruler of your country. What you need is money. You have a money factory – a 'mint'. The coin-makers want you to design your coins. On the 'heads' side will be a picture of your handsome head with words around the edge telling the world how great you are.

On the 'tails' side of the coin can draw anything you like – if you enjoy flying kites then you may want a picture of a kite. If you like fish-fingers it may be a fish with fingers.

Draw two large circles (around a cup maybe) and design the heads and tails of your coins.

2. RUTHLESS RULES

Now you are the ruler (with your own coins) you need to make sure you make clear and fair laws.

Write down TEN laws... and maybe punishments for people who break your laws.

Here's an example:

LAW 1: *When I do a piece of school work I want 10 out of 10 every time. Any teacher who gives me 9 will have a finger snipped off, two fingers for 8 out of 10 and so on. Any teacher who gives me 0 out of 10 will never pick their nose again.*

(I didn't say they had to be SERIOUS laws... but they can be if you want.)